FLYING FERGUS

The Best
Birthday Bike

First published in Great Britain in 2019 by
PICCADILLY PRESS
4th Floor, Victoria House, Bloomsbury Square
London WC1B 4DA
Owned by Bonnier Books
Sveavägen 56, Stockholm, Sweden
www.piccadillypress.co.uk

This is a work of fiction. Names, places, events and incidents are either
the products of the author's imagination or used fictitiously. Any
resemblance to actual persons, living or dead, is purely coincidental.

A CIP catalogue record for this book is available from the British Library.

ISBN: 978-1-4714-0521-1
Also available as an ebook and in audio

14

Typeset in OpeDyslexic-Alta
Printed and bound in Great Britain by Clays Ltd, Elcograf S.p.A.

Piccadilly Press is an imprint of Bonnier Books UK
www.bonnierbooks.co.uk

FLYING FERGUS

The Best Birthday Bike

CHRIS HOY

with Joanna Nadin

Illustrations by Clare Elsom

Piccadilly
PRESS

CONTENTS

Meet Fergus

and his friends...

Fergus

Grandpa Herc

Mum

Wesley Wallace

Daisy

Chimp

Choppy Wallace

Dermot Eggs

Meet Princess Lily

and her friends...

Princess Lily

Demelza

Douglas

Dimmock

Prince Waldorf

Hounds of Horribleness

Chapter 1

The Sullivan Swift

Fergus Hamilton was an ordinary eight-year-old boy. He liked football (when his team won), fish fingers and chocolate cake (only not on the same plate), and his dog Chimp (when he wasn't eating socks or chewing the stairs). He didn't like broccoli (but he ate it), or homework (but he did it), or the way his mum left lipstick on his cheek when she kissed him goodnight (but he didn't complain).

1

Yes, he was ordinary in almost every way, except one. Because, for a small boy, Fergus Hamilton had an extraordinarily big imagination.

Some days he imagined he lived in an enormous underground lair, with fifty-seven bedrooms and a hover car and a butler to serve him lemonade whenever he wanted it, instead of in the flat above his grandpa's junk shop on Napier Street.

Some days he imagined he could build a time machine out of a vacuum cleaner, like Captain Gadget, his favourite comic book superhero. Then he could defeat his own arch-nemesis Wesley Wallace. Wesley didn't have a hover car but his house was massive and he was definitely allowed lemonade whenever he wanted.

Some days Fergus imagined Chimp
was a sleek and well-mannered
pedigree hound who could sniff out
buried treasure and catch criminals,
instead of a mongrel with matted
fur and a tendency to dig for bones
in the carpet.

But mostly Fergus imagined he
was the most brilliant boy cyclist
in the whole wide world, because if
there was one thing he liked more
than football, or chocolate cake,
or even Chimp (especially when he
was chewing Fergus's socks), it was
cycling.

On this particular wet Friday
afternoon, his nose pressed against
the glass of Wallace's Wheels,
Fergus was imagining he was Steve

4

"Spokes" Sullivan, champion cyclist, world record holder and the brains behind the Sullivan Swift.

The Swift had twenty-four gears, hydraulic brakes and state-of-the-art suspension. It was, without doubt, the most beautiful bike Fergus had ever seen.

CLOSED

SULLIVAN SWIFT!

THE SULLIVAN SWIFT
GRAB YOUR CHANCE TO RIDE LIKE STEVE SPOKE

He imagined shooting down Craigmount Hill on it, so fast he would feel the wind taking his breath away. He imagined careering up a ramp then taking to the air for a few short seconds of flight that would feel like minutes.

Most of all Fergus imagined hopping out of bed tomorrow morning on his birthday, seeing an enormous parcel in the front room and unwrapping it to find a Swift inside, along with a new helmet, gloves and a special racing jersey. Then he might, just might, be able to join Wallace's Winners, the best cycling team in the city.

Wallace's Winners had come first in the Great Cycle Challenge

five years running. Fergus wasn't
keen on the fact they were coached
by Choppy Wallace, former district
champion, owner of Wallace's Wheels
– and father of Wesley. Fergus was
especially not keen on the fact that
Wesley was their number one racer.
But if it meant getting a step closer
to being like Spokes then Fergus
knew he just had to get on the team.

"In your dreams, loser," said a
voice behind him.

Fergus jumped and turned to see Wesley Wallace whizz past on the latest and most expensive edition of the bike, the Swift Superior.

Fergus sighed. Wesley used to have a Swift Elite, but it got scratched from being dumped on the pavement all the time, so his dad had given him a new, even better one.

Fergus's dad wasn't a cycling champion, or any kind of champion. Fergus didn't actually know what his dad was because he'd disappeared before Fergus was born.

Sometimes Fergus liked to imagine his dad had been kidnapped by aliens. Sometimes he thought

he might be working undercover
as a secret agent. And sometimes
his grandpa said his dad had got
trapped in a parallel universe called
Nevermore, fighting a duel with the
dreaded King Woebegot.

Mum said he'd probably just
moved to Kilmarnock, and to stop
filling Fergus's head with far-fetched
stories because there were enough
in there already.

Fergus sat back down in the
saddle of his rusty but trusty bike
Old Faithful, and began pedalling
back down Napier Street towards
home.

Wesley may be annoying, he
thought, but he was right, it was

never going to happen. He was
never going to make Wallace's
Winners, and he was never, never,
NEVER going to be like Spokes
Sullivan.

Not on this old thing, anyway.

Old Faithful may be trusty, but
she was way too old and way too
small. He'd had her since he was
just a wee boy, so now every time
he turned the pedals his knees
knocked his elbows and his elbows
stuck out like chicken wings.

There was no way he could do
a wheelie or a bunny hop on this
bike without getting tossed over
the handlebars or tangled in the
spokes.

It was no good, Fergus decided,
he needed a Swift, and he needed
it now.

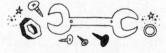

"Och, love," said Fergus's mum
at tea. "I wish I could afford it,

but I'm already doing all the shifts the hospital can give me, and I've bought your presents. Anyway, you've got a bike."

"But, Mum," protested Fergus. "I look like a loser on it. Everyone says so."

"Daisy doesn't say so," said Grandpa.

"That's only because she hasn't got a bike at all," said Fergus. "Because she's not allowed to cycle any more because her mum says it's too dangerous."

"Her mammy thinks breathing's dangerous," laughed Grandpa.

"Exactly," said Mum. "So think yourself lucky." And she popped the last fish finger on his plate with a smile.

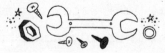

Fergus lay in bed that night and thought about what Mum had said. He was lucky, he supposed. He had Grandpa, and Chimp, and a mum who wasn't too scared to let him climb trees or graze his knees. He had a brilliant best friend in Daisy, and even though she didn't have a bike she knew all about them from the books she borrowed from the library and from Fergus's magazines.

Plus it was his birthday tomorrow and he was bound to get some good presents, even if none of them was a Sullivan Swift.

But still, he couldn't help feeling hard done by.

He picked up a tattered copy of *In The Saddle* magazine next to his bed and turned to the interview with Spokes.

Interview with
SPOKES
SULLIVAN

"Bikes are in his blood," says Spokes Sullivan's coach Champ Lamington.

"When he gets the itch to pedal, he's just got to scratch it."

Spokes agrees with his Aussie boss: "My mum said I should have been given two wheels instead of feet."

"The only time I'm really happy is when I'm in the saddle. Or reading it, of course!"

IN THE SADDLE NEWS · · · · · · · · ·

But could Spokes's reign as world champ be coming to an end? Turn to page 15 for our profile of up and coming cycle star Dan "Dandy" Doolittle. His performance in the Tour of Scotland has certainly got tongues (and tails) wagging.

"Some people are born champions," Fergus whispered to Chimp, "and some people are born losers. You and me, I guess we're losers. What do you reckon?"

Chimp thumped his tail on the floor and then started eating a shoe.

"Yup," sighed Fergus. "Losers."

Chapter 2

The Birthday Surprise

That night Fergus dreamed again
he was Spokes Sullivan, beating the
world record by the skin of his teeth
and riding down the home straight
to the sound of the crowd clapping
and cheering and shouting his name.

So, when he woke up at silly
o'clock the next morning, he jumped
out of bed and into the front room
hoping to see a giant, Swift-shaped

package propped against the fireplace.

There wasn't one.

"Maybe it's hidden in the airing cupboard," he said to Chimp.

It wasn't.

"Maybe it's under the sofa," he guessed.

It wasn't.

"Maybe it's . . . in the fridge?" he tried.

It wasn't. But there was a plate of his favourite marmalade sandwiches, so he took one and bit into it.

"Fergus Hamilton, you wee beastie," said his mum as she came through the door in her nurse's uniform, back from the night shift. "They're for tea later."

"Sorry," said Fergus through a mouthful of marmalade.

"Och, it's only one and it's your birthday, anyway!"

Mum hugged Fergus so tight he dropped the rest of the sandwich, much to Chimp's delight who swallowed it, along with a piece of chalk and a plastic soldier.

"By jinks, Fergus, you're up
with the crack of dawn." Grandpa
shuffled into the kitchen rubbing
his eyes. "It's not even six yet."

"He's been looking for his
presents," said Mum.

"Have not!" fibbed Fergus.

"Pants on fire," Mum said, and
smiled. "They're in the cupboard
with the vegetables. I knew you'd
never look there."

"Oh . . . great," said Fergus, but
he felt his heart sink knowing there
was no way anyone could squeeze
a bicycle in with the spuds and the
swede.

He was right. In the cupboard
were three parcels, but not one was
big enough to be even a scooter.

There was a box of toffees from
Mrs MacCafferty who lived two
doors down and had a cat called
Carol that terrorised Chimp.

There was a pack of playing cards
with star footballers on the back
from Mrs Flynn who lived two doors
up and had a cat called Colin that
terrorised Carol.

And there was a book about
Spokes Sullivan from Mum, along
with a kite and a card that played
"Happy Birthday" in seventy-three
languages.

"They're all fantastic," said
Fergus. "Thanks." And he meant
it, because he loved toffee and
playing card games and he'd
always wanted a kite. "I'll put
them in my bedroom," he said. "For
safekeeping," he added, eyeing
Chimp, who was eyeing the toffee.

"Hang on, sonny," said Grandpa.
"You haven't opened mine yet."
And he handed Fergus a square
cardboard box.

Fergus shook it and it rattled
slightly. Then he carefully unfolded
all the flaps until he could see
inside.

It was a bike helmet. A brand-new,
shiny, red and yellow bike helmet.

"That's . . . brilliant," said Fergus.

"Well, try it on, sonny," said Grandpa.

"Maybe later," Fergus said, thinking there wasn't much point trying it on ever.

"But safety comes first and you're going to need it."

"Er, for what?" asked Fergus, confused.

"For this," said Mum and opened the front door to the flat.

There, on the landing, was a package. A tall, wide, almost-definitely-bike-shaped package.

"I don't believe it!" cried Fergus. And he didn't. How had she managed it? They didn't have the money for a Swift, he knew that, and yet . . . right in front of him, wrapped in brown paper with a tag hanging off the handle, was a bike.

"Happy Birthday, Fergus," the tag
read. "Love Mum and Grandpa."

Fergus went to work, ripping
off the brown paper in strips,
Chimp barking happily at his side,
until standing there, in front of
him, was . . .

Well, what exactly was it? Because its paintwork was a rusty brown, it had barely eight gears, and there was no suspension to be seen. One thing was for sure, though, it most definitely was *not* a Sullivan Swift.

"Er . . . thanks," said Fergus, unable to hide the disappointment in his voice.

"I know it's not the one you wanted, love," said Mum. "But it works, doesn't it, Herc?"

"Aye," said Grandpa. "More than. Do you know this was your dad's bike back in the day? He even beat Choppy Wallace on it once."

But that was years ago, thought Fergus to himself. Now it didn't look as if it could beat Chimp.

"It's been in the back of my shop all that time and I'd forgotten it until now," said Grandpa. "Lick of paint and it'll be good as new. Come on, let's go and give it a spin."

"I'll . . . I'll try it later maybe," said Fergus. "I'm a bit tired. I think

I did wake up too early after all. I might just go back to bed for a bit."

Quickly and quietly he took his other presents back to his bedroom and flopped onto the duvet, leaving the bike standing forlornly in the front room with Mum and Grandpa.

Fergus fell asleep and dreamed he was Captain Gadget saving the world with an anti-forcefield deflector made out of a kettle. Too late! The forcefield had ricocheted onto the princess and sent her into a deep sleep. "Wake up!" he cried into her ear. "Wake up, wake up, wake up."

"Wake up," echoed the princess.

"Wake up, wake up, Fergus."

Hang on. Fergus? That wasn't right. Fergus opened an eye. And sighed. There on his bed was Daisy, eating a marmalade sandwich and wearing his new helmet.

"It's beast, this," she said, swallowing. "The helmet, I mean – the sandwich is okay but I prefer chocolate spread and peanut butter."

"I guess."

"You guess? You're crazy, Fergus Hamilton. I suppose you think this is a pile of old junk, too," she said pointing at the bike, which was now leaning against his wardrobe.

Fergus's heart sank when he saw it again. "It IS a pile of old junk, Daisy."

"Are you kidding? It's a bike, Fergus. A BIKE. And okay, so it might not have twenty-four gears or fancy suspension, but that makes it pretty

lightweight – I've tested it and even
I can lift it. Plus, IT'S A BIKE!"

"But . . ."

"Butts are for sitting on, that's
what your grandpa says. Come on,
we just need to clean it up and paint
it and maybe add some bits here and
there and take a few others off."

"Well . . ."

"Wells are for falling down. Come
on, just give it a try. Haven't you
always said that one day you want
to build your dream bike?"

Fergus nodded. He had, it was true.

"Now's your chance. And you can

put this on it too." She handed
Fergus a tiny packet.

He opened it. Inside was a luminous,
circular thing with a dial.

"Er, thanks," said Fergus. "What is
it?"

"Like, duh. It's a glow-in-the-dark
compass bell. All the best bikes
have them."

Fergus grinned. Daisy was right.
Grandpa was right. He had a bike. A
BIKE! It just needed some love, and
a few adjustments, that was all.

"Then we'd better stick it on then,"
said Fergus. "Come on, we've got
work to do!"

Chapter 3

Test Run

Fergus, Daisy and Grandpa worked hard all morning. By the time Chimp started thinking he might be ready for a sausage or two, the bike had been transformed.

Daisy had scrubbed off the dirt and sanded off the rust, Grandpa had given it new pedals from a set he'd got off a racer in his junk shop, the brakes had been checked, the

chain and gears oiled, and finally
Fergus had painted it bright, glossy
orange.

"It looks BEAST!" said Daisy,
fastening the glow-in-the-dark
compass bell to the handlebars.

"And just in time, too."

"Time for what?" asked Fergus.

"For the tryouts for Wallace's Winners, of course," said Daisy, shaking her head. "There's a poster up in Wallace's bike shop. They're recruiting a new member and the tryout's next Sunday."

Now it was Fergus's turn to shake his head. "But I haven't got the right shorts. And Wesley hates me. And –"

"And nothing," interrupted Daisy. "Who cares what shorts you wear, as long as you're fast?"

"She's right," added Grandpa. "If you're good enough, and I know you will be, they'd be fools not to take you."

"But if I'm NOT good enough, then I'll be the one looking like a fool," Fergus pointed out.

"Well, you won't know until you try, will you?" said Grandpa. "So what do you say we pop to the park and give it a spin?"

Chimp barked happily at the sound of the word "park". And Fergus knew there was no way he could resist both Chimp AND the chance to see if he really did have Spokes's potential.

"Okay. You're on," he said.

"Let's go," Daisy said, already halfway out of the gate. "Last one there's a numpty."

When they got to the grassy slope at the top of Carnoustie Common, Fergus strapped on his helmet and settled into the saddle, the tips of his toes touching the ground. He took a deep breath. This was the moment he'd been waiting for: those few seconds before you set off. He could feel his heart start to beat harder in anticipation.

"Make sure you keep pumping," said Grandpa. "You'll need to get up to a fair old speed if you're going to get round the Middlebank tryout track in time."

"How will I know when I'm going fast enough?" asked Fergus.

"You'll know," said Grandpa. "Because it feels . . . it feels like you're about to fly."

"Beast!" said Daisy.

"Can I go now?" asked Fergus, itching with impatience.

But Grandpa wasn't quite done. "One more thing," he said. "When you do get that flying feeling, try not to freewheel, and don't, whatever you do, let the pedals spin backwards."

"Why? What will happen?" asked Fergus.

"If this was a track bike you'd fall off. Their pedals don't spin back at all," said Daisy knowledgably. "I learned that off the telly."

"But this isn't a track bike," said Fergus.

"I know," said Grandpa. "But you'll lose your focus, you might spin out of control and, och, just don't do it, okay?"

"Okay," replied Fergus, thinking that pedalling backwards sounded pointless anyway.

"I'll time you," added Daisy, finger poised over the stopwatch button on her wristwatch. "Ready? On your marks, get set . . . GO!"

Fergus pushed down on the right pedal and felt himself move off. He wobbled at first, the bike unsteady on the grass, but as he picked up pace his path seemed straighter, and he felt stronger and surer.

He pushed down harder on the pedals, again and again, the wheels bounding off the bumpy turf, and Fergus bouncing in the saddle.

"Faster!" he heard Daisy cry.

"Faster!" called Grandpa.

"Yeah, faster, Hamilton," called another voice. "You loser."

Fergus whipped his head round. Standing next to the climbing frame was Wesley Wallace, along with his sidekick Dermot Eggs, who had a shaved head and a permanent scowl.

"You'll never make the Winners," shouted Wesley.

"Yeah, never," added Dermot, pointlessly.

"Just watch me," Fergus muttered.

No sooner had he said those words than the bike hit a tussock causing his foot to slip off the pedal.

"Aargh!" cried Fergus as the bike veered to the right. Then "Eeeeek!" as it veered to the left.

Then CRASH! Fergus slid off into the sandpit and the bike landed in a heap next to him.

"Nice one, loser," laughed Wesley, standing over him.

"Yeah, nice," echoed Dermot.

"No chance you'll make our team,
Hamilton. You're slower than a snail
pulling a rock."

"Yeah," sneered Dermot.
"A snail."

"Shove off," said Daisy who had
arrived, panting, at the sandpit,
Chimp panting harder beside her.

"Happily," sneered Wesley.

"Yeah," said Dermot. "Happily."

"Are you his parrot?" asked Daisy.
"You sure sound like one."

At that, Dermot stuck his hands

in his pockets and slunk off behind
Wesley.

Fergus watched them, knowing
his cheeks were as red from
embarrassment as they were from
the effort.

"Are you all right?" asked Daisy.

"I'm fine," he snapped.

"That was some ride," said
Grandpa, who had finally caught up.

"Yeah, some ride," sighed Fergus.
"I was slower than a snail, and
then I fell off. I knew this bike was
rubbish. We shouldn't have bothered
doing it up. It's a waste of paint."

"It's not the bike that's the problem," said Grandpa. "Even on a Sullivan Swift you'd have been lucky to go much faster. You just need to practise. That's what it's all about. No such thing as magic, just hard graft."

"I'm a born loser, though," said Fergus. "I'll never do it, even if I practise every day."

"Och, Fergus. No one's born a winner or a loser," said Grandpa. "Not even Spokes Sullivan. Sure, he's got talent, but that's just the beginning. Without working at it he'd just be a regular fellow with a fancy bike."

"I don't even have that," moaned

Fergus, looking forlornly at the tangled heap in front of him.

"Fancy enough," said Grandpa. "And anyway, you've got something that Wesley and Dermot definitely don't have."

"What's that?" Fergus asked.

"Imagination," said Grandpa. "You dream big, just like your daddy did. So pick the bike up, dust yourself off and go again. And again. And again. Until you do it. Because you will, sonny. I know you will."

Daisy nodded furiously. "Come on, Fergus," she said.

Fergus looked at Chimp, who licked Fergus's face happily, then spat out a mouthful of sand.

"Maybe just once more, then," he said. "Just the once."

Chapter 4

Flying Fergus

So Fergus tried it again, just the once. And then a second time. And a third. And then he came back after school the next day, and the next, until it was the weekend again and he was spending every free minute he had up on the common.

"Hurry up, Fergus," said Daisy, as he fiddled to get the saddle height just right for the tenth time that

Saturday morning. "The tryout's tomorrow and we've only got an hour left to practise!"

"Okay," replied Fergus. "Keep your hair on!"

But he wasn't cross really. Because riding his new bike was the most fun he'd had in, well, forever. Every go felt faster than the last. And this time he would do it for sure.

Fergus knew he just needed that last little push.

Grandpa had said: "When your lungs are burning and your heart's pounding and your legs feel like they can't go another inch, turn it up."

Maybe he couldn't "ride like he was being chased by evil knights", which was Daisy's suggestion, but he could definitely turn it up, and he would.

"Ready?" Daisy asked.

Fergus put his foot on top of the pedal and leaned forward. "Ready," he replied.

"On your marks, get set . . . GO!" she called.

And he was off, this time with Chimp bounding and barking after him. Fergus leaned low on the handlebars like Daisy had told him to, making himself more streamlined. He pulled his elbows in too, and he'd already made sure all his clothes were as tucked in as possible.

Now it was down to his legs. They
were pumping furiously. He was
nearly there. He pumped harder.
And harder.

"Come on!" he said to himself,
as the grass below became a blur
of mossy green. "Just a little more."

"Nice one, Fergus!" called Daisy.
"I reckon you can slow down now."

But Fergus wasn't really listening
and he definitely wasn't going to
slow down. He was almost there,
he could tell. He could feel it in his
heart and in his head.

Fergus felt like Captain Gadget
zooming through the air with a jet-
pack strapped to his back. He felt
like Spokes Sullivan soaring round
the velodrome in a blur of wheels
and blue team strip.

Fergus closed his eyes and gave
it that last shot of power. And then
he felt it: the wind on his face,
the vibrations in the handlebars, a
soaring in his heart – he was flying,
really flying.

And that's when it happened.

53

First, he stopped pedalling. And then, without thinking, he let his feet turn backwards on the pedals once, twice, three times. There was a tiny flash and a sound like the crack of a faraway firework, but Fergus was too caught up in the joy of the ride to hear anything but himself.

"Whoop!" he yelled, and opened his eyes, hoping to see Daisy cheering him to the finish line.

But something was wrong. There was no sign of Daisy. In fact there was no sign of the park at all! Fergus looked to the left. Then to the right. Then he looked down.

Oh, holy mackerel! he thought to himself.

Because he really WAS flying. Only that didn't look like the park below him. Fergus peered down, desperately trying to make out anything familiar.

"I'd watch where I was going if I was you, mate," said a voice behind him in a gruff Australian accent.

"Huh?" Fergus swung round and there, clinging on to the saddle, was what looked like . . . "CHIMP?"

"Yup, last time I checked," replied the dog. "But seriously, mate, eyes on the prize or we're going to –"

CRASH!

Fergus felt himself hit the ground for the second time.

Only now he wasn't sure which ground it was, or where.

Chapter 5

Nevermore

Fergus gazed at the scene around
him: the castle up on the hill in the
distance, the seam of mist hanging
between that and the forest below,
then the lush green clearing in which
he seemed to be sitting.

"Where . . .?" he began, a thousand
questions whirling in his head.

"No idea, mate," replied Chimp.

"And why . . .?" Fergus asked.

"Beats me." Chimp shrugged.

"But . . . how?"

"Portal to another world? Magic pedals? Too much cheese before bed? Take your pick."

"And before you ask," the dog went on, I haven't the first clue about the accent, but I reckon it suits me."

"But you're . . ."

"A dog? I know."

"But I don't understand. I mean, normally you're just chewing stuff."

"Looks like chewing to you, but me, I'm testing it for radioactive chemicals, poison, gold . . ."

"Really?" Fergus looked flabbergasted.

Chimp laughed. "Nah, mate, it just tastes good."

Fergus tried to take it all in. This couldn't be happening, could it? It had to be his crazy imagination. "Is . . . is this a –"

"Dream?" finished Chimp. "I don't know, mate. Maybe she can tell you."

Chimp nodded over Fergus's
shoulder and Fergus swung round
to see a girl his own age, dressed
in a gold-tasselled gown, a tiara
and mismatched wellington boots.

The girl was staring at Fergus as if he was the odd-looking one.

"Who are you?" she demanded. "Did Prince Waldorf send you? Are you . . . spying on me?"

"No," replied Fergus. "I was just racing my bike on the common and then, well, there was this sort of a flash and –"

"What he means," interrupted Chimp, "is it's bonzer to make your acquaintance, Miss . . .?"

"Lily," said the girl, smiling now. "Well, Princess Lily, to be exact."

"Fergus," said Fergus. "To be exact. And this is Chimp."

"Pleasure to meet you." Lily grinned in a decidedly non-princessy manner. Then stopped. "Hang on, did you say *bike?*" she asked.

Fergus nodded. "There." He pointed at the orange heap behind him.

"Oh. My. Goshness!" Princess Lily's eyes popped out on stalks. "A Hamilton Herc?"

"Huh?" said Fergus. "It's not anything. I made it myself. Well, with my grandpa and my friend Daisy. And how did you know my surname?"

"I've heard of these," said Princess Lily, ignoring him and busily

admiring the spokes and saddle instead. "But I've never seen one. I thought they'd all been destroyed when the ban came in."

"The ban?"

"The cycling ban, duh!" said Lily, not sounding at all princessy at that point.

"Cycling's banned here?" asked Fergus, worriedly.

"Only since forever," replied Lily. "Well, maybe not forever. But ever since King Woebegot fell off his bike in the middle of the championship race and decided it was too dangerous."

"More like the bozo was embarrassed," snorted Chimp.

Lily grinned again. "You know, you're just as smart as you look," she said. "He is a bozo. But he's also the meanest man in four kingdoms, and, worst of all, he's my dad."

Before Fergus could say anything, Princess Lily went on. "Not that Mum's much better. She thinks the whole WORLD is dangerous and that princesses should stay at home and paint their toenails all day. BO-RING."

"I'll say," said Fergus.

"Anyway, the point is," said Lily,
"no one's allowed to ride any more.
Not EVEN Precious Prince Waldorf,
my twin brother. But you, on the
other hand, must be pretty nifty
on that thing." She nodded at the
bike.

"Well, yes," admitted Fergus. "But
you just said cycling was against the
law."

"True," said Lily. "But I don't see
the law around here right now, do
you?"

"I . . ." began Fergus.

"Go on," begged the princess.
"Give us a show. I've never seen
anyone ride one, not in real life."

"Of course he will," Chimp
answered for him, slapping him
on the back with a paw.

Fergus spluttered. "But . . ."

"Butts are for sitting on," said Lily. "Didn't anyone ever tell you that?"

Fergus nodded. Someone had, only –

"Then let's get cracking." Princess Lily interrupted his thought. "If my history books are telling the truth, this needs a bit of attention, though."

Princess Lily was looking closely at Fergus's bike. "And of course we'll definitely have to make a few additions."

"Additions?" asked Fergus.

"Sure," she answered. "I mean, where's your stealth shield?"

"My what?"

"And your jet booster?" added Lily. "And your smoke generator, your oilslicker and your chocolate button dispenser?"

"Chocolate button dispenser?" repeated Fergus.

"Okay, so I was joking about that

one," laughed Lily. "But you really can't ride round here without them."

The princess paused, then said, "Not with all the . . . 'obstacles', shall we say?"

"Obstacles? What kind of obstacles?" demanded Fergus.

"Oh, nothing to be worried about," started the princess. "Just the odd dragon, a flying monkey or two. The usual, you know?"

Fergus shook his head. He didn't know at all. But still, the chance to ride a bike with a stealth shield and a smoke generator? Not even he could have imagined that in his wildest dreams.

Maybe it really was just that – a dream – in which case, he might as well make the most of it before he woke up.

"You're on," he said. "Let's do it."

Chapter 6

The Swamp of
Certain Death

The bike was ready in what seemed
like seconds to Fergus. What was
more incredible was that Chimp did
half the work and had all of the
tools they needed.

"What? You didn't know that dogs
had pockets?" Chimp said.

Fergus didn't know what he knew
any more. Just that he wanted very

much to ride the newly adapted –
what was it Lily had called it? The
Hamilton Herc? Fergus wanted to
ask her again about that name but
there was no time right now.

"Now remember," said Lily, "it's
more about being alive than being
fast. Not that I want to worry you."

"Oh, you're not," assured Chimp.

Oh, she is, thought Fergus.

"So it's a lap of the Enchanted
Forest," began Lily. "Past the Well
of Everlasting Torment, through the
Gruesome Glade – watch out for the
serpents there – then ending on the
other side of the Swamp of Certain
Death."

"Cer-Cer-Certain Death?" stammered Fergus.

"Yeeees," said Lily. "But only nine out of ten people actually die, and I've got a feeling you're one of the lucky ones."

"Of course he is," said Chimp, slapping Fergus on the back again before he could protest.

"You hope so, anyway," said a sneering voice.

They turned to see a blond boy wearing a silver suit with a cape and hovering above them in some kind of flying golf buggy. Next to him, in the passenger seat, was a thuggish-looking sidekick dressed all in black.

"Waldorf," sighed Lily. "And Dimwit. What are you doing here?"

"His name's Dimmock," snapped Waldorf, though Dimwit certainly seemed to suit him more, thought Fergus. "And you know it. What's more, you know cycling's against the law."

"She's not cycling," said Chimp.
"He is." The dog pointed at Fergus.

Thanks a billy bunch, thought
Fergus as Waldorf stared at him.

"Him?" laughed Waldorf. "This
peasant? This nincompoop? This
LOSER?"

"Hey, that's my boy you're talking
about, mate," said Chimp. "And he's
pure-bred champion."

"What, like you, mongrel?"
sneered the prince.

It was Fergus's turn to stand
up for his friend. "You leave
Chimp alone, he's the best dog
in Scotland."

"We're not in Scotland," snorted Waldorf. "Wherever that is. We're in Nevermore. Or hadn't you noticed?"

Fergus felt his stomach slip and a strange, cold feeling slide through his bones. "Did you just say . . . N-N-Nevermore?"

"Y-Y-Yes!" mocked Prince Waldorf. "I assume you HAVE heard of it?"

Fergus nodded slowly. That was just it, he had heard of it, in Grandpa's stories. And what's more –

"Oh, honestly, Waldorf," said Lily before Fergus could ponder any further. "Everyone knows you'd ride a bike if you got half a chance."

"Would not," argued Waldorf. "Not when I've got my Handy Hover 3000." He patted the hovermobile, which just then let out a puff of dirty smoke.

"Would too," coughed Lily.

"Whatever," said Waldorf. "Though I must admit, I am keen to watch the boy in action. I always like to see a spectacular swamp-sucking in the afternoon. Builds up the appetite."

"Oh, do put a sock in it, Wally," said Lily.

"Or better, a boot," said Chimp.

Fergus would have giggled if he hadn't been so, well, terrified.

Lily turned to Fergus now. "You will do it, won't you, Fergus. Please?"

Fergus was beginning to have second thoughts. And third ones. "I . . ."

"Pretty please with peanut butter and chocolate chips and a marshmallow on the top?" she begged.

"Of course he will." Chimp slapped Fergus on the back. "Now come on," the dog continued. "Focus, Fergie. Eyes on the prize, remember?"

"Eyes on the prize," echoed Fergus. Though right now he wasn't sure what the prize was or where to look for it.

"Now do you remember how all the buttons work?" asked Chimp.

Fergus nodded. Although he was struggling to work out which one was the stealth shield, and which were the smoke generator, the dragon distractor, the annoying music and the cloud of grasshoppers.

"And you can only use one of them, so pick carefully," said Lily.

"Oh, okay," said Fergus.

"Because you definitely don't want to use the puff of pink glitter when what you really need is the bunny hopper," she said. "Believe me."

Fergus believed her.

"Okay. On your marks . . ." announced Lily.

Fergus pressed his foot against the pedal.

"Get set . . ."

He leaned forward, ready.

"GO!"

And he was off, pedalling furiously towards the Well of Everlasting Torment. What was it that Daisy had said? Wells are for falling down? Well, he wasn't going to let that happen to him.

Fergus gave the well a wide berth, leaning inwards as he cornered on the edge of the trees that made up the track's edge.

Next up was the Gruesome Glade,
and its serpents.

No sooner had he thought it than
an ugly creature, more than a metre
long, slithered across his path,
causing Fergus to swerve.

"Hang on!" called Lily.

"Keep going!" yelled Chimp.

Fergus righted the bike but saw
that another two serpents were
heading his way, fast. He could use
the stealth shield, he thought. But
he only had one chance – what if
he needed another button later?
No, best to just slalom in and out of
the creatures like the bollards
at the park.

He pushed the bike left, then
right, weaving in and out of them
as they darted across the floor of
the glade.

"Done it!" yelled Lily.

Not yet, thought Fergus. *Not until I'm through the Swamp of Certain Death.* He gulped. In front of him the grass gave way to mud that oozed and bubbled noisily.

Fergus focused on the path between the pools. "I'll stick to that," he said to himself. "Can't go wrong."

But as he headed down the path, a puddle appeared in front of him. "Yikes!" he screeched and wobbled out of the way. "It's a moveable swamp!"

"Scaredy cat!" he heard Prince Waldorf shout. "Yellowbelly . . . LOSER!"

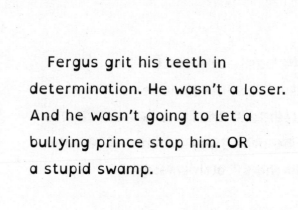

Fergus grit his teeth in
determination. He wasn't a loser.
And he wasn't going to let a
bullying prince stop him. OR
a stupid swamp.

This was the time for a button.
Only which one?

Fergus looked at the panel in front of him. That one was the glitter, and that was water. Or was it the other way around? And where was the stealth shield?

Fergus hovered one finger over the red buttons. He was running out of time, a gulping great hole of gloop was opening in front of him. There was only one thing for it: he was going to have to take pot luck!

"Here goes nothing," he said, and pushed hard on the third button from the right.

Princess Lily gasped, Chimp covered his eyes with his paws, and Dimmock and Waldorf sniggered to themselves.

But as the front edge of his wheel began to slide into the gunk, the bike suddenly jumped two metres into the air and cleared the entire bog.

Bunny hops! thought Fergus. *Brilliant!*

He hit the ground just as another bubbling chasm opened up in front of him. But he quickly pressed the button and again the bike jumped into the air and cleared. Then again and again, until Fergus found he had bounded over the finish line.

Fergus braked hard and jumped off the bike before it could decide to take flight for another time.

"You did it!" cried Lily running up
to congratulate him.

Fergus blushed as she hugged him.
"It was . . . nothing," he said, not
wanting to boast.

"Are you kidding?" she said. "You
were incredible."

"Lucky, more like," snorted Prince Waldorf.

Chimp ignored him. "Immense," he told Fergus.

"Beast!" agreed Lily. "If King Woebegot saw you do that, maybe he'd change his mind about cycling."

Fergus flicked a glance to Waldorf.

The prince shrugged. "Yeah, and pigs might fly."

"I hear monkeys do," said Chimp.

"And dogs." Lily grinned. "So you'd better come back."

"But –" began Fergus.

"Butts are for sitting on,"
interrupted Lily. "Besides, you
HAVE to. This is a Herc," she said,
touching the handlebars of his bike
with reverence. "Official cycle of the
Heroes."

"The Heroes?" asked Chimp.

"Didn't I tell you about them?"
said Lily.

Fergus and Chimp shook their
heads.

"The rival cycle team that beat
the king. They were called the
Heroes." Lily smiled. "Hamilton's
Heroes."

Chapter 7

The Knights of
No Nonsense

Fergus felt his tummy flip and his
heart jump for what felt like the
bazillionth time that day.

This was one coincidence too
far. So the bike was named after
Grandpa Herc, the land was called
Nevermore, and now the team was
Hamilton's Heroes – his very own
surname?

But how? And why?

Lily answered before he could manage to get the words out. "Named for their captain – the man who beat King Woebegot in the race," she said.

It couldn't be, could it?

"And what . . . what happened to him?" asked Fergus.

"No one knows," replied Lily. "But he's probably locked in the Dungeon of Despair. Or banished to the Desert of Dementia."

"Or slunk off back to whatever weird land he came from," sneered Waldorf.

"He couldn't," said Lily. "They confiscated his bike."

"She's right," said Dimmock. "It was flung into the firepit with the dragons."

"Shut it, Dimwit," said Waldorf. "No one asked your opinion."

Dimmock shut it. But Lily didn't.

"All that's left is the bell," she continued, "which the king keeps in a glass jar in his study."

Fergus's head swirled with possibilities. Maybe this wasn't a dream. Maybe Nevermore wasn't such a far-fetched story. Maybe his dad wasn't in Kilmarnock after all.

"When did this happen exactly?" he asked, hardly daring to hope for the answer.

"Nine years ago," said Lily. "Or rather nine years last week."

Nine years! That would be just before Fergus was born. Just before his dad disappeared . . .

"I —" But before he could get another word out, a cannon shot thundered out across the forest.

"Oh, rats!" cried Lily. "It's the Knights of No Nonsense.

"The w-w-what?" stammered Fergus.

"And the Hounds of Horribleness," added Waldorf, smiling. "You're in BIG trouble now."

"Come again, mate?" yelped Chimp.

"The . . . oh, never mind," said Lily. "No time. You need to get out of here before they catch you with that bike. But promise me you'll come back?"

"You haven't even seen the
Cliffs of Catastrophe yet," Princess
Lily went on. "Or Douglas, my pet
dragon. Plus I REALLY want a go
on the Herc!"

"I . . ." Fergus thought for a
moment. He couldn't really say no
to a princess, could he? Plus he
had his own reasons for wanting to
see more of the kingdom, even if
he was happy to give the Cliffs of
Catastrophe a miss.

"Okay," he said. "I'll come back. I
promise."

"Beast!" exclaimed Lily. She
turned to Waldorf. "And if you blurt
a word of this to Dad or Mum I'll
tell on you for letting Dimwit drive

that hovermobile. You know he's
not passed his test."

Waldorf turned to Dimmock. "I
told you she'd catch you. You . . .
DIMWIT!"

Dimmock opened his mouth to
protest but Lily interrupted. "Much
as I'd like to see you two twits in
one of your tiffs, I think avoiding
death is *slightly* more important."

Fergus turned his head to hear
the unmistakable sound of some
very horrible hounds closing in.

"I think it's time to –" he began.

"SCRAM!" finished Chimp.

In a matter of seconds, Princess Lily had skedaddled one way and Prince Waldorf and Dimwit had hovered off the other, leaving Fergus and Chimp alone in the clearing. Fergus heard another howl and the roar of motorbikes getting closer.

"What do we do, Chimp?" he wailed.

"You're asking me?" said Chimp.
"You're the one who got us here."

"But how?"

"Maybe you said a secret password
accidentally?" offered Chimp.

"Good idea!" said Fergus. "Let's
give it a go. Open sesame!" he yelled.

Nothing happened.

"Abracadabra!"

Nothing happened.

"Sausage sandwiches!" tried Chimp.

Still nothing happened.

"Sausage sandwiches?" asked
Fergus. "Those are magic words?"

"They are to me, mate," replied
Chimp.

"Well, they're not working," said
Fergus. "Nothing is."

Another howl sounded out across
the forest, closer now.

"Quick. You need to think back," said Chimp. "What were you doing before we ended up here? Like, were you crossing your fingers and wiggling your nose at the same time?"

"No!" said Fergus. "This is hopeless. I wasn't doing anything at all. I was freewheeling!" He paused. "Hang on. That's it! I just need to get up to speed and let my feet spin the wrong way and we'll be home!"

"Sounds fishy to me," said Chimp.

"Well, it can't be worse than standing here saying 'sausage sandwiches' and then getting squished to smithereens by the Knights of No Nonsense, can it?"

"Fair dinkum," said Chimp. "Let's go."

And so, with Chimp clinging onto the crossbar, Fergus set off on a straight path into the woods.

"Faster," yelled Chimp as the sound of a hunting horn trumpeted behind them.

Fergus bent down over the
handlebars, his legs pumping up
and down like pistons. He was
nearly there.

"Come on!"

The Hounds of Horribleness were
closing in. Fergus could hear their
panting and smell the meat on their
breath. Grandpa's words came back
to him. "No such thing as magic. Just
hard graft." He could do it. He had to.

Even though his heart was pounding
and his lungs hurt with every breath,
he dug deep, really deep, and, just
as one of the hounds leapt into the
air to pounce, he shut his eyes, gave
it that last push and let his feet spin
backwards once, twice, three times . . .

WHOMP! The bike hit a bush and Fergus spun off to one side and Chimp and the bike to the other.

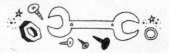

"Fergus!" cried a girl's voice. "Are you okay?"

"Princess Lily?" Fergus pulled himself up on one elbow and opened an eye.

"Who in the whole of the Highlands is Princess Lily?"

Fergus smiled, then his smile widened into a massive grin. "Daisy!"

"That's my name, don't wear it out," she replied. "Did you hit your head or something?"

"No, I . . ." Fergus touched his
helmet to make sure. "I don't think
so. What time is it?"

"About one minute later than it was the last time you asked." Daisy stuck her hands on her hips. "Before you decided to break the land speed record."

"You mean . . . I've been here all the time?"

"Are you sure you didn't hit your head? Maybe we should postpone the tryout. Though that would be a shame as you totally nailed it!" Daisy smiled.

Fergus had a sudden thought. "Oh no. Where's Chimp?"

Daisy nodded towards the bush. "Digging for sausages."

At the magic word, Chimp bounded

out of the bushes, flopped down on Fergus's feet and started licking his shoe.

"Chimp . . ." began Fergus. "Did you . . . can you ... say 'mate'?"

"Right, that's it," said Daisy. "Either you're concussed or this is all a very weird dream."

"You think this is weird?" said Fergus. "You should have come on the bike with me."

"I'd rather have my own bike," sighed Daisy.

"I know," said Fergus. "I wish you had your own bike too. I can give you a backie if you like, though?"

"I reckon you've done enough riding for one day. You need to save yourself for tomorrow," said Daisy. "Maybe we should all walk."

"Yeah, you're right," agreed Fergus. "We've had way too much excitement already, haven't we, Chimp?"

Chimp looked up from the shoe, wagged his tail, and snapped at a fly.

No one would believe me if I told them, thought Fergus, as they wandered home across the park. *I'm not even sure I believe me. But I know one thing: I believe IN me now. I can pass the tryout tomorrow. I know I can.*

Chapter 8

The Tryout

"Are you ready?" asked Grandpa
as he checked the brakes for the
umpteenth time that morning.

"Ready as I'll ever be," said
Fergus, tightening the strap on his
helmet, before having one long,
last look around him at the famous
Middlebank track. This was where
Wallace's Winners trained. This
was where Spokes had trained.

113

Now Fergus Hamilton was getting
the chance to join them. As long as
he could make it round fast enough,
that was.

"Good luck," said Daisy.

"Yes, good luck, sonny," said
Grandpa. He looked across the track.
"Are those your school friends over
there, here to cheer you on?"

Fergus followed his gaze past the
other hopefuls and their mums and
dads to where Wesley Wallace and
Dermot Eggs were sitting astride
their Sullivan Swifts with the rest
of their team, great smirks on their
faces. Just his luck they'd be here
watching the tryout.

"Jeer me on more like," said
Fergus quietly.

"Focus on what you're doing,"
said Grandpa. "It's about you, not
about them."

"So, 'Hamilton' is it?" said another voice.

Fergus looked round. It was Choppy Wallace, stopwatch in his hand.

"That's right – Fergus Hamilton," said Grandpa.

"Think he's got what it takes, do you, Herc?" asked Choppy.

"I know he's got what it takes," replied Grandpa.

"Let's hope he's got staying power too, then," said Choppy. "Unlike his dad," he added.

Fergus saw his grandpa's face redden.

"Lucky for you, Choppy," said Daisy, "or you wouldn't have been district champion, would you?"

It was Choppy's turn to get red in the face and Fergus feared it would be all over before it had even begun. "Shall we get going?" he piped up.

Grandpa nodded quickly. "Good idea."

"Fine," said Choppy, coldly. "It's one lap, and Mikey McCloud has already done it in two minutes three seconds, so you'd better be quicker than that."

Two minutes, three? thought Fergus to himself. That was going to be tough. Impossible even.

"Nothing's impossible," said
Grandpa, reading his mind.

Choppy snorted. "Any shortcuts,
you'll be disqualified. Any tricks,
you'll be disqualified. Any arguing –"

"He'll be disqualified, we get it,"
said Daisy.

Choppy shot her a look.

And no pedalling backwards,
Fergus thought to himself. That was
the last thing he needed right now.

"Right, on your marks . . ." cried
Choppy.

Fergus took a deep breath.

"Get set . . ."

You can do this, he told himself.
*It's not the bike that's magic, it's
you. Hard graft. That's what it takes.*
Fergus poised his foot on the pedal.

"GO!"

And he was off, steady and
straight and building up speed
at a spectacular rate.

"Come on, Fergus!" called Daisy.
"Give it some welly!"

He did, pushing his feet down
harder with each revolution. Left,
right, left, right, until they became a
blur below him. He whizzed past the
halfway mark.

"On the home straight!" shouted
Grandpa. "Hamilton strikes again!"

Fergus focused on the finish line.
He had just yards to go and seconds
to do it in.

But what was that? Dermot Eggs
had dropped his bike in the middle
of the track. If Fergus steered
around it, it would cost him vital
time.

Fergus looked frantically at his handlebars. Where was the bunny hop button? Or the puff of glitter? Or the dragon distractor? He gulped. It really was down to him. No magic here, just what he had inside him.

He pulled to the right and pedalled
for all he was worth, swinging back
just in time to cross the finish line
and pulling up sharp to the cheers
of Daisy and Grandpa, and the happy
barking of Chimp.

"Did I do it?" Fergus asked Choppy breathlessly. "Did I?"

Choppy held out the stopwatch. He didn't need to say anything. Fergus could see for himself. Two minutes, ten. He was out, way out.

"But that's unfair," protested Daisy. "Dermot put his bike in the way deliberately. The DIMWIT."

"You don't know that," said Choppy.

Oh, I do, thought Fergus.

"I get it," said Grandpa. "You
just can't stand the thought of a
Hamilton on the team, can you?"

Choppy's face tightened.

"Well, that's easily solved," said
Grandpa. "We'll start a team of our
own."

"You?" spluttered Choppy.

"Why not? I know bikes. I can fix
them up."

"But, you're . . . you're . . ."

"Brilliant!" finished Daisy.

"And amazing!" added Fergus.

Grandpa smiled. "What do you reckon then, kids? Our own team?"

"Can I be on it?" asked Daisy.

"We'd have to get you a bike first, and get permission from your mammy."

Daisy's face fell. "And monkeys might fly."

"They might," said Fergus, quickly.

Grandpa laughed. "Now that would

be a sight. What Fergus means is, we'll do everything we can to help. And until then, you can be assistant coach. Will that do you?"

Daisy nodded eagerly.

"Fergus, you're our number one rider," announced Grandpa. "We'll need to recruit some others, but I reckon you're a pretty good start." He winked.

"What will we be called?" asked Daisy.

"Oh, I don't know," said Grandpa.

"I do," piped up Fergus. "I know exactly what we'll be called."

"What?" asked Daisy.

"Yes, what?" asked Grandpa.

"Hercules' Heroes," Fergus blurted out. "It's perfect, isn't it?"

Grandpa smiled. "That's nice of you, Fergus. But we're not heroes just yet. Not until we win. How about . . . Hercules' Hopefuls? Bit more modest, eh?"

Fergus nodded. "Hercules' Hopefuls," he repeated. "I like it."

"Hercules' Halfwits more like," said Wesley.

"Now, now," said Choppy, but he had a smirk on his face.

"Well, I wish you luck, Hamilton. You're going to need it. My Wesley's a born champion if ever there was one."

"No one is born a champion," replied Grandpa. "And it's not about luck –"

"It's about hard graft," finished Fergus, smiling.

"You said it, sonny," Grandpa said.

Choppy shook his head. "Maybe we'll meet you in the heats of the Great Cycle Challenge then . . . in ten years. When you can afford a decent bike." He laughed.

"Make that next month," said
Grandpa. "And we'll be sticking to
the bike we've got, thanks. Won't
we, Fergus?"

Fergus looked at his bike,
shining bright and orange in the
sun. It might not be expensive,
and it might not have twenty-four
gears or fancy suspension, but it
was his, he'd helped build it and
so to him it really was the best
bike in the world, ever.

"We will," he said. "We definitely
will."

Chapter 9

Dreaming Big

As he washed mud off the spokes of his bike's front wheel, his legs aching nicely and a huge grin on his face, Fergus thought how quickly life had turned around.

Just a week ago Fergus didn't even have a bike that was big enough for him. Now he had one that could fly, a dog that could talk (even if it was in an Aussie accent)

and, what's more, he might, just
might, have found his missing dad.

Fergus looked at Grandpa sitting
in the old green chair reading his
Evening News. He'd talked about
Nevermore, hadn't he? So Grandpa
had to know the truth.

"Can I ask you something, Grandpa?" he blurted.

Grandpa looked up from the sports pages. "What's that, Fergus?"

"That place you used to tell me about – Nevermore," said Fergus. "Is it real?"

"Nevermore?" Grandpa looked baffled. "Oh, wait, I remember. That old bedtime story. Why are you asking about that all of a sudden?"

Bedtime story? Fergus struggled to hide the disappointment that washed over him. "No reason," he lied.

"Och, Fergus," Grandpa sighed.

"You want to find your daddy, don't you?"

Fergus nodded. "I just . . . I want him to see me ride."

"And that's a sight I'm sure he'd love to see," said Grandpa. "But, as for Nevermore, if it helps to imagine your daddy's there, well, I'm not going to stop you, sonny. But remember this: I'm here," said Grandpa. "Right here, in the real world. And so's your mam. And we love you."

"I know," said Fergus. "You're right. And I know I'm lucky."

"Aye, you are. And that's a true Hamilton speaking." Grandpa smiled.

"Which is a good thing, because
we've got important work to do in
the morning."

"What's that?" asked Fergus.

"Have you forgotten already?"
laughed Grandpa. "Finding enough
kids with bikes to be on our team.
And persuading Daisy's mammy to let
her be one of them. But right now
it's bedtime, sonny. Off you go."

So off Fergus went, trudging
slowly up the stairs to his bedroom,
Chimp trailing behind him.

"I can't believe it," said Fergus as
he flopped onto the bed. "I honestly
thought it was real."

Chimp said nothing, just started
scratching at something bothersome
on his side.

"Maybe I just wanted it so badly
I made the whole thing up. Yeah,
that's probably it. I made it up. I
imagined it was happening just like
I imagine I'm Captain Gadget. Don't
you reckon, Chimp?"

Chimp didn't even seem to know

what "reckon" meant, but he did give a happy bark as whatever had been bothering him detached from his fur and rolled along the floor.

Fergus sighed and leaned over the edge of the bed to see what it was, and found his sigh turning into a sort of gurgled gasp.

Because right there, on his bedroom floor, was a gold tassel. What's more, it was exactly the kind of gold tassel that had been at the bottom of Princess Lily's dress.

"Chimp, you . . . you . . . GENIUS!"

Fergus snatched the treasure up and held it tight in his hand, as if he was holding on to hope itself.

Because, at that precise moment,
he was holding on to hope. The
hope that one day soon he'd be a
cycling champion. And, better, that
somehow he'd be able to tell his
dad all about it.

And he was holding on to dreams, too. Only this time he wouldn't have to imagine he was Captain Gadget, or even Steve "Spokes" Sullivan. He'd be plain old Fergus Hamilton.

All of a sudden, that didn't seem quite so boring after all.

Sir Chris Hoy MBE, won his first Olympic gold medal in Athens 2004. Four years later in Beijing he became the first Briton since 1908 to win three gold medals in a single Olympic Games. In 2012, Chris won two gold medals at his home Olympics in London, becoming Britain's most successful Olympian with six gold medals and one silver. Sir Chris also won eleven World titles and two Commonwealth Games gold medals. In December 2008, Chris was voted BBC Sports Personality of the Year, and he received a Knighthood in the 2009 New Year Honours List. Sir Chris retired as a professional competitive cyclist in early 2013; he still rides almost daily. He lives in Manchester with his family.

www.chrishoy.com

Joanna Nadin is an award-winning author of more than seventy books for children, including the bestselling Rachel Riley diaries, the Penny Dreadful series, and Joe All Alone, now a BAFTA award-winning TV series. She studied drama and politics at university in Hull and London, and has worked as a lifeguard, a newsreader and even a special adviser to the Prime Minister. She now teaches writing and lives in Bath, where she rides her rickety bicycle, but she never, ever back-pedals...

www.joannanadin.com

Clare Elsom is an illustrator of lots of
lovely children's books, including Maisie Mae
and the Spies in Disguise series. She is also
the author-illustrator of Horace and Harriet.
She studied Illustration at Falmouth University
(lots of drawing) and Children's Literature at
Roehampton University (lots of writing). Clare
lives in Devon, where she can be found doodling,
tap dancing and drinking cinnamon lattes.

www.elsomillustration.co.uk

This brilliotic book about Fergus and his friends is set in a reader-friendly font and design, for maximum enjoyment for everyone.

The font we have used is called OpenDyslexic. You can find out more about it here:
www.opendyslexic.org

Dyslexia affects as many as 1 in 10 people, and often makes reading more difficult. We wanted to make our books as easy to enjoy as possible, so this special font and a design with lots of space helps us do just that.

Not everyone with difficulty reading has dyslexia, and not everyone with dyslexia has the same difficulties. You can find out more about dyslexia on these wonderful websites:

The Dyslexia Association: **dyslexia.uk.net**

British Dyslexia Association: **bdadyslexia.org.uk**

Dyslexia Scotland: **www.dyslexiascotland.org.uk**

PRESS

Thank you for choosing a Piccadilly Press book.

If you would like to know more about our
authors, our books or if you'd just like to know
what we're up to, you can find us online.

www.piccadillypress.co.uk

And you can also find us on:

We hope to see you soon!